Keeping Secrets

Adapted by Beth Beechwood

Based on the television series *Hannah Montana*, created by Michael Poryes and Rich Correll and Barry O'Brien

Part One is based on the episode written by Michael Poryes

Part Two is based on the episode written by Douglas Lieblein

Bath · New York · Singapore · Hong Kong · Cologne · Delhi · Melbourne

First published by Parragon in 2007
Parragon
Queen Street House
4 Queen Street
Bath BA1 1HE, UK

ISBN 978-1-4075-0240-3

Printed in UK

Part One

Chapter One

The crowd was going wild after the Hannah Montana concert. But all Hannah could think about was getting offstage and taking off her wig! Then she could go back to being Miley Stewart. Miley was so glad she hadn't told her friends that Hannah Montana – the pop star they were all crazy for – was really just her in disguise! She enjoyed knowing that her friends liked her for who she was, not because she was famous. Only her dad, her brother and her best friend, Lilly, knew the truth.

"Clear the way, clear the way! Superstar coming through!" Miley's dad, Robby Stewart, shouted to the crowd as he, Miley and Lilly hurried toward the limo. They all had to wear disguises in order to protect Miley's secret. Lilly was dressed as her alias Lola Luftnagle and carrying a little Goth lapdog named Thor. Mr Stewart was in his 'Hannah's manager' disguise.

Miley, still dressed as Hannah Montana, always made sure that she showed her appreciation to the fans. She turned to the crowd and smiled broadly. "Thank you, everybody!" Her strong voice carried the words like a song. "Love to you all! See you next time!"

Though Lilly knew how popular Hannah was, it always surprised her to be in the thick of it. "This is totally insane!" she said.

Then, holding Thor up to the crowd, she yelled, "Back off, people! Back off – don't make me release Thor!"

"Yeah," Miley said, smiling at her brave defender. "You go get 'em, Thor. Two pounds of pure piddle just lookin' for a target."

Looking down and nodding at the puddle surrounding his feet, Mr Stewart said, "Actually, I think he just found one."

Lilly was embarrassed. "Oh, man!" she cried as they piled into the limo and closed the door. But the window was still half open and they could hear someone shouting, "Hold up! Wait!" It was Oliver Oken, Hannah Montana's number-one fan.

"Oh no," moaned Miley. "It's Oliver. *Again*. He sneaked into my dressing room last week. He nearly climbed onstage the week before. Just when I think he can't get any more obsessed, *bam!*, he kicks it up a notch!"

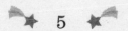

Mr Stewart was entertained, though. "Look at those bony little elbows go!" he said as Oliver made his way through the throng. "That boy cuts through a crowd like a lawnmower."

Miley was anxious. "Close the window!" she commanded. Lilly responded swiftly and the window almost zipped shut, but not before Oliver could thrust his hand inside and stop it from closing all the way.

"Hannah, please!" Oliver begged. "Kiss my hand and I'll never wash it again."

Miley rolled her eyes. "Looks like he never washed it now." Thinking fast, she took Thor from Lilly and pointed him at Oliver's grimy hand. "Come on, Thor, make yourself useful."

Thor gave Oliver's hand a big lick. Fooled, Oliver was beside himself. "Oh, baby, that was a wet one!"

Even when Miley slapped Oliver's hand out of the way, he was not discouraged.

"Ooh, I like 'em feisty," Oliver swooned as he pulled his hand away. Lilly was able to close the window at long last, and Mr Stewart turned to the driver.

"You can head out," he said.

Miley was exasperated. "Man," she sighed. "He's never gonna give up."

Lilly got serious. "You'd better hope he does. Because if he ever finds out your secret, he'll not only be in love with Hannah Montana, he'll be in love with you!"

Miley looked at her friend incredulously. "What? That's crazy! The only thing that's the same about Hannah Montana and me is–" Miley paused for a moment until she realized the truth, "–me." She gathered herself again. "And 'me' doesn't feel that way about him!"

Her dad, however, quickly reassured her. "Don't worry, Mile, I know guys and sooner or later he'll get tired of chasing after someone who doesn't chase back." But they all realized it would probably be later rather than sooner. This was Oliver they were talking about. And everyone knew Oliver never gave up.

Just then Mr Stewart opened the window only to find Oliver furiously peddling his bike alongside the limo. He clutched a small bouquet of flowers in his hand and as they began to disintegrate in the wind, he shouted, "Do a dude a favour and don't get on the motorway!" But the limo sped up and Oliver finally started to fall behind, throwing the flowers through the limo window in a last-ditch effort to impress Hannah. "For you, my love!"

Miley shook her head at Thor. "Why did you have to be such a good kisser?"

 8

Chapter Two

The next day at Rico's, a beach hangout, Oliver was holding court with all the guys, telling them the tall tale of Hannah's hand kiss. Miley and Lilly had just arrived from the beach, when they overheard Oliver's story. Even Chad the Chomper, who had been busy shooting hoops, stopped long enough to listen.

"It's true," Oliver insisted to the guys. "Hannah actually kissed this hand," he said, pointing to an imaginary spot.

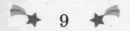

"You've gotta be kidding me," said one of the guys he was talking to.

Oliver would not entertain doubters. "A big, slobbery wet one," he said enthusiastically. "Look, it's still shiny."

Lilly couldn't resist. She whispered to Miley, "Yeah and now every time Oliver calls my house, my dog goes, 'Is it for me, is it for me?'" The girls giggled at their inside joke.

"Chad, dude, close up shop when you chew," Oliver demanded. Chad was chomping on chewing gum a little too dramatically for Oliver's liking. "You're getting spit on the Hannah hand!" Chad wasn't about to listen to Oliver, though. Instead, he shoved another piece of chewing gum into his mouth and chewed even louder. Oliver moved his hand away to protect his precious doggy kiss.

Lilly had had enough. "Mile, let's go.

You're cutting into my tan time."

But Miley was distracted. "Look at him, he's never gonna quit. What happens if he does find out? I really care about Oliver. It'd totally weird out our friendship."

Lilly became a little suspicious of her friend, suddenly. "Unless deep, deep down, maybe, just maybe, you feel the same way . . ." They both glanced over at Oliver, who was busy stroking the side of his face with the part of his hand Hannah had kissed. The image shook Miley back into reality. "Yes, and maybe, just maybe . . . that's insane!" They laughed and looked on as Oliver continued with his fantasy story.

"Now that she's left her mark on me, it's time to take our relationship to the next level," Oliver said. "Tonight at her CD signing, I'll stare into her eyes and say, 'You're my love, my life, someday you'll be my . . .'" He paused for a moment and stared at the sky, deep in thought. Then he started to write on his hand, *"Note to self: think of word that rhymes with 'life'."* Just then, one of the guys pointed out something pretty crucial to Oliver.

"Dude, isn't that the Hannah hand?"

Oliver screamed, "AHHHHH!" Looking sorrowfully down at his hand, he pined, "Forgive me, my love."

The whole incident reminded Miley of something she had forgotten, too. "The CD signing! If he stares into my eyes, he might totally recognize me."

Lilly didn't buy it and brushed off the possibility. "It's never gonna happen."

Miley was still concerned. "But what if it does?"

Lilly looked at her friend seriously. "Then you'll learn to love him like I did with my brother's hamster. And here's the beauty part: if Oliver dies, you won't have to bury him in your back garden."

Sometimes Miley couldn't believe she even knew Lilly. "When you talk, do you hear it, or is there, like, this big roaring in your ears?"

Meanwhile, Oliver was getting more and more irritated as Chad chewed his gum. Chad, clearly amused by this, moved even closer to Oliver's ear and chomped even louder.

"Back off, Chad!" Oliver yelled.

Chad agreed. "Fine. Throw this away for me, would ya?" With that, Chad took the wad of chewing gum from his mouth and slapped it down, right on Oliver's precious Hannah hand.

Oliver couldn't take it. "Get it off," he screamed. "Get it off!"

One of the guys to whom Oliver had

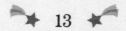

been bragging earlier looked on curiously. "What's the deal with you and chewing gum?" he asked Oliver.

Suddenly Oliver was lost in the blurry past. He was back in his cot. He was a baby and all he could remember was an older woman, his Aunt Harriet, leaning over him, chomping on gum. *Chomp, chomp, chomp.* "Look at you, little Ollie," he recalled her saying while she chomped. "Aunt Harriet wants to eat you up." *Chomp, chomp, chomp.* "You're just so yummy, darling . . . yummy, yummy, yummy."

Oliver cringed as he remembered what had happened next. Aunt Harriet's gum had fallen right out of her mouth with the last "yummy" – right out of her mouth and onto a very disgusted little Ollie. Oliver shook himself back to the present at Rico's.

"I hate that woman," he said out loud to no one in particular.

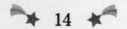 14

Chapter Three

While Miley and Lilly were at the beach and Oliver was shaking off the babyhood memory that had scarred him, Mr Stewart was on the sofa at home, busy writing songs.

"... Been sittin' here all mornin', tryin' to write a song – can't remember when it took me this dang long ... maybe I should just up and fly the coop ... 'cause everything I'm writin' sounds like –" Thankfully, he was interrupted by Miley's older brother, Jackson.

"I got it, Dad! Prepare to be blown away," Jackson announced dramatically.

Mr Stewart pretended to be annoyed. "This had better be good, son, I was in the middle of a masterpiece."

Jackson put on the voice of a game show host to get his father in the mood for his big news. "Jackson Stewart, come on down!" he bellowed. "You are the proud new owner of a brand-new used car! Yes, over the last fifteen years, this pre-owned beauty's been driven by heavy smokers, sloppy eaters and one Wilma McDermott, whose cat popped out six kittens on the front seat – yes, some stains just don't come out!" Jackson finally finished his performance and looked at his dad for a reaction.

"And you're happy about that?" Mr Stewart asked. Jackson gave it one more shot in his game-show voice. "Yes, I am!"

Then he turned serious. "Dad, it's my own car that I bought with my own money."

"I'm proud of ya, son. Especially that 'my own money' part," he said with a smile as he patted his son on the back. "Let's go take a look at that puppy."

"Ooh, puppies," Jackson said as they walked outside. "That reminds me, on the back seat—"

Mr Stewart cut him off. "I don't want to know."

They got to the driveway, where they saw a red convertible. Jackson continued to make a very big deal out of his very big purchase. "Bup-bup-bup-baaaaa!" he sang out proudly.

"Well, would you look at that," Mr Stewart nodded as he walked around the car, inspecting it carefully. "Clean, no dents and . . . yep," he said after checking out the front seat, "there's that stain." Just then, Jackson's friend, Cooper, ran up the driveway to meet them. He looked around, puzzled and excited at the same time.

"Where is it?" Cooper demanded of Jackson.

"Right here," Jackson said.

"This?" Cooper asked with a laugh.

Jackson completely understood his friend's doubt. "I can't believe it's mine either," he said.

"And I can't believe you just bought a girl car!" Cooper blurted out.

"What?"

Cooper took a step towards his friend to explain. "Jackson, only girls drive this thing. It's a chick-mobile, a babe bucket, a skirt scooter – you might as well have bought a bra with tyres, man."

Jackson wouldn't have it. "You are so

wrong. This is totally a guy's car. When I was driving home, there were guys honking, waving and . . ." he slowed down, realizing why he'd received so much attention, ". . . giving me kissy faces . . . oh, no." Jackson looked at his dad for solace. "Dad, tell me I didn't just buy a chick car," he pleaded.

Straight-faced, Mr Stewart replied, "You didn't just buy a chick car."

Jackson didn't believe him. "Now say it like you mean it," he demanded.

Leaning in through the driver's window, Mr Stewart said, "I'd like to, son, but–" The car bleated out a too-cute *toot-toot*! Mr Stewart couldn't resist. "You know how ladies like to have the final word."

Chapter Four

Later that night, after the CD signing, Miley's usual entourage piled into the limo. Once again, they had to fight the crowd. Miley was dressed as Hannah, of course, and Lilly and Mr Stewart were decked out in their 'costumes', too. Even Thor was in his little doggy-Goth getup again.

Mr Stewart fought to close the door as Miley shouted, "Thanks for coming! Love you! Love you all!" The door slammed shut.

"Okay, driver," Mr Stewart said. "Let's boogie."

Miley excitedly whipped off her wig. "That was great! Oliver looked right into my eyes and never had a clue."

Lilly nodded. "Kind of like the look he has in Spanish." She laughed. The two girls turned to each other and imitated the slightly confused, but mostly blank, stare Oliver always had in Spanish class. "*No comprendo!*" they yelled in unison.

"I don't know what I was so worried about, anyway," Miley said as she settled back and relaxed.

Mr Stewart opened the sunroof to let in some fresh air.

"Ahh!" They all screamed as Oliver's head popped into the limo from above. Thinking quickly, Miley grabbed Thor and put him right in front of her face. Immediately, her father put her wig back on, albeit slightly askew.

"Don't be scared!" Oliver announced. "It's me, Oliver Oken!"

Mr Stewart was not pleased. "Driver, pull over!" he demanded.

"Wow, you're even more beautiful upside down," Oliver said to Miley as he hung from the roof.

"Well, thank you," Lilly replied. Miley gave her friend a look.

"He was talking to me," she said. Then she looked up at Oliver and pleaded, "Look, you're very sweet, but you have to stop doing this because . . ." Miley paused, trying to come up with a reason he should stop. *What would make him stop all this?* She had it. ". . . because I have a boyfriend!"

Oliver was visibly stunned. "A boyfriend?" He looked hurt. "I don't understand. Then why did you kiss me?" he asked.

Miley sighed and picked up Thor. "I

didn't kiss you," she explained. "He did."
Well, if no one else had a thing for Oliver,
Thor certainly did. As soon as Miley held
him up to Oliver, he started licking Oliver's
face furiously.

Oliver was mortified. "Oh, man. Those
are the lips I've been thinking about for the
last twenty-four hours?"

Miley felt bad now. "I'm sorry," she said.
"I was trying not to hurt your feelings, but
I'm just not interested. Okay?" She was
trying to be as careful as possible with her
fragile friend.

"Okay," Oliver moped. "I get it."

Mr Stewart stepped in. "That's good,
son. Now get off this roof before you dent
it. This is a rental."

"Fine," Oliver replied. "I won't bother
you any more."

Lilly tried to help ease his pain. "If it

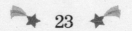

helps, the dog hasn't stopped talking about you," she said hopefully.

Oliver was clearly upset. "You must think I'm pathetic," he said to Miley.

"No," she said gently. "I think you're sweet. And maybe, if I didn't have a boyfriend . . ."

"I'd have a chance with you!" Oliver interrupted her with his old gusto.

Miley tried not to panic. "I never said that," she said anxiously.

"But you implied it!" Oliver wasn't going to let her off the hook now. "And that's enough! I'll wait for you forever!"

"I never said that!" Miley cried. But it was no use. As Oliver pulled his head out of the sunroof, she could hear him shouting . . .

"Forever! Do you hear me, Hannah Montana?! Forever!" His voice finally faded away.

Lilly was relieved. "Man, that was close," she said to Miley. "He almost caught you tonight."

"Ya think?" Miley said with extreme sarcasm in her voice. "Why do I have to be so irresistible?"

Mr Stewart piped up with a solution he had been pondering. "You know what that boy needs?" he asked the group rhetorically. "A *real* girlfriend."

Miley started to dismiss her father's idea. "Dad, that is . . ." Then, as she spoke, she realized he might be right. "That is the smartest thing you've ever said!" she shouted gleefully.

Mr Stewart nodded. "Yeah, well, every now and again even a blind pig snorts up a truffle."

Lilly raised her eyebrows. "And that's the weirdest."

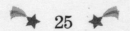 25

Chapter Five

The next morning at school, a kid struggling to open his locker called out to Oliver. "Yo, Locker Man!"

"I'm on it," Oliver said confidently. And without even breaking his stride, he pounded on the corner of the locker. Just like that, the sticky door flew open. Oliver could fix a stuck locker better than anyone.

"I owe you," the kid said gratefully.

"I'll be back to collect," Oliver replied

over his shoulder as he headed towards his next gig.

"Locker Man," a girl in distress called to him. This would be easy. Oliver spun himself around and elbowed the centre of the girl's locker, which popped right open. "You're amazing, Oliver," she cooed.

"I've been told that," Oliver winked. Then he noticed Chad passing by. "Having trouble with your locker, Chad?" he asked smugly.

"Yeah," Chad grunted.

"Well, Locker Man is on the job," Oliver said. "B-But not for you, *sucka*." Just then, Miley approached Oliver. She was about to put her dad's plan into action.

"Oliver, see that girl, Pamela, over there?" she asked, pointing to a pretty girl across the hall. "She thinks you're cute." Miley prayed he'd take the bait.

"Can't say that I disagree," Oliver shrugged. "Too bad I'm already cruisin' down the Hannah Highway."

Miley looked down the hallway and spied another girl for Oliver. "What about Kyla Goodwin? She's so desperate, she'll go out with anybody," Miley insisted.

Oliver considered this option. "Usually my type of woman, but I'm taken," he said.

Miley was getting desperate, until she spotted Lilly approaching them. She pulled her friend over to them. "Hey, how about Lilly?! You guys would be perfect together."

Lilly was not happy with Miley at this moment. "Excuse me?" she asked.

Miley forged ahead with her plan, despite the likelihood that Lilly might kill her later. "You're both stubborn," she pointed out.

In unison, Oliver and Lilly said, "I am not!"

"You always agree with each other," Miley said.

"No we don't," the two of them answered.

"Yes," Miley nodded. "I am definitely seeing a couple here."

Oliver and Lilly turned to each other, overlapping their words, "You're not? Because I'm not . . . phew."

Miley liked where this was going. She changed her plan, mid-course. "And that's smart," she said, referring to the fact that the two friends weren't actually interested in each other that way. "Because what if one friend loved another but didn't get loved back?" she asked earnestly. "Then things would get all weird and the friends couldn't be friends any more." She paused. "And nothing is more important than our friendship, Oliver,"

Miley said slowly, hoping he would get it.

But Oliver didn't get it at all. "Oh, man!" he shouted. "You love me!"

"No!" Miley said quickly. "I mean, I do love you, but like a brother, or . . . a pet fish." She was fumbling for the right words. "I mean, I'd cry if I had to flush you down the toilet, but I don't want to kiss you." She prayed she was making herself clear.

"That's a relief," Oliver replied. "Because you're my buddy and I think Hannah and you could wind up being close friends," he said seriously.

Lilly muttered, "Closer than you think."

"Great! Once Hannah and I are together, we'll have you out to the island." Oliver was getting more and more worked up as he talked. "We're going to get an island!" Miley banged her head against a locker in frustration. Then she and Lilly watched as

Oliver practically skipped away from them towards his locker.

With just a few taps, his locker promptly popped open. He was Locker Man, after all. Inside was a picture of Hannah. "Soon, my love, we'll be together," he swooned. Only this moment between Oliver and his picture of Hannah didn't last long. Chad the Chomper just couldn't leave it alone. He stretched the wad of chewing gum out of his mouth until it reached Oliver's precious Hannah, sticking it right on her. Then he pulled the rest of the wad from his mouth and let it dangle from poor Hannah's likeness.

"This isn't over, pal!" Oliver shouted as Chad walked off. Then, turning to the picture, he said, "Goodbye, Hannah 102," and he pulled the picture off his locker. "Hello, Hannah 103!" he said, staring at the exact same picture of Hannah.

Lilly and Miley witnessed this whole incident. Then Lilly got a certain mischievous look in her eye. "I know that look," Miley said. "Either you have a great idea or you've really gotta go."

"Oliver is about to totally get turned off Hannah Montana," she said, and then paused. "And I really gotta go!"

Chapter Six

Jackson Stewart couldn't care less about what was going on with Miley, Lilly and Oliver. He had much bigger things to worry about. He and his dad had just pulled into the driveway in his chick-mobile. "I can't believe he wouldn't take the car back," Jackson said to his dad. "I thought I made a very convincing argument."

Mr Stewart gave his son a look. "Technically, getting on your hands and knees and begging is not an argument," he explained as they both got out of the car.

"Hey there, neighbour," a voice called out to them.

"Oh, man, it's Mr Dontzig," Jackson said. "And he's in a dressing gown again."

Mr Dontzig was the Stewarts' neighbour and he was known for being underdressed and over-involved in neighbourhood concerns.

"Count your blessings," Mr Stewart said. "At least this time it's the long one." Mr Dontzig approached them on the driveway, revealing his whole outfit: the long dressing gown over a baggy swimsuit and a pair of flip-flops on his feet.

"So, Stewart family," he started. "What would another leaf from your tree be doing in my hot tub?" He held up the guilty leaf.

"Oh, I don't know," Mr Stewart smirked.

"Maybe it wanted to party."

Mr Dontzig was not amused. "Well, something needs to be done about this."

Mr Stewart stared at his neighbour's belly and retorted, "And something needs to be done about *that*. I'm suggesting either some sit-ups or a bigger dressing gown."

Jackson pointed to his dad enthusiastically. "Zing!" he shouted.

Mr Dontzig turned to Jackson's car. "Nice ride, Jackson," he said. "My wife used to have a car like this. Traded it in. She thought it was too girly." He paused and then said, "Get your leaves out of my pool!" He started to leave, but Mr Stewart wouldn't let the gruff neighbour have the last word.

"I'll have you know, we Stewart men don't define ourselves by the kind of cars we drive," he said proudly as Mr Dontzig walked off. But to Jackson, his father muttered, "That's it, this dolly wagon's going back to where it came from." And with that, he hopped into the driver's seat.

"But the salesman already said no," Jackson explained.

"To you," Mr Stewart said. "Not to me. Face it, son, I'm a little bit more intimidating." He started to back out of the driveway but accidentally hit the horn. *Toot-toot!* "Lord!" he cried. "If I have to choose between that and an accident, I'm taking the accident."

Chapter Seven

Later that day, Lilly and Miley were about to put Lilly's plan into action. Lilly had called Oliver and told him to meet her at a remote part of the beach. She had also shared some startling news about Hannah Montana. Now Lilly was hiding behind a big rock, waiting for Oliver to arrive.

Oliver came running up to her. Breathlessly, he said, "I came as fast as I could! Is she still here?"

Lilly pointed to Miley, who was in

Hannah mode. "Right over there."

"I can't believe you saw Hannah Montana break up with her boyfriend right here on our beach, at the exact moment I was getting home from the orthodontist."

"I know," Lilly said in her best faux-dramatic voice. "Knock, knock, who's there? Fate."

"Fate who?" Oliver never understood Lilly's sense of humour.

"Just go!" Lilly commanded.

Oliver gathered himself. He had to get psyched up for his moment. "Okay," he said, breathing deeply. "This is it . . ."

"Good luck, Oliver," Lilly bubbled. "But remember, if it doesn't work, you're still 'Smokin' Oken',"

"Thanks," Oliver answered. "But it's gonna work out."

"Absolutely!" Lilly assured him. "But if it

doesn't . . . Smokin' Oken. 'Nuff said."
Lilly walked away and Oliver headed
bravely towards his destiny.

He approached Hannah, who was sitting
with her back to him. "Hi, it's me, Oliver,"
he said. "I heard about your breakup and
I'm here for you. If you need a hug, my
arms are open." This was all very nice of
course, sweet, even. If only he had actually
said it to Hannah! The 'girl' who had had
her back to him turned around to reveal
that she wasn't Hannah Montana at all.
She wasn't even a girl. She was a he.

"Get away from me, you pasty-faced
little freak!" the guy shouted.

Oliver retreated. "I can do that," he said
as he backed away carefully. Then he
spotted another blonde girl with her back
to him. This time, he was more careful.
"Hannah?" he asked.

Miley, as Hannah – giant sunglasses, blonde wig and all – was chomping on a giant wad of chewing gum. When she turned to Oliver, her cheeks were positively swollen and she was drooling. "Hey, the kid from the sunroof," she slurped.

Oliver was stunned. Put off, even. "Whoa," he said as she shoved yet another piece of chewing gum into her very crowded mouth.

"Where are my manners?" Miley exclaimed. "Sit down, sweetie, join the party." She grabbed Oliver and put him in her chair. "You want some gum? Here." She handed him a packet of bubble gum. "Load yourself up."

"I didn't know you liked gum," Oliver stammered. "I've surfed all of your websites and none of them said you were a chewer." He didn't quite know how to process this new 'wad' of information.

"Oh," Miley said, chomping right in Oliver's face, "I love to chew. I chew all the time. Like a train – chew, chew, chew." As she chewed, chewed, chewed in his face, Oliver suddenly couldn't get the image of Aunt Harriet out of his head. Miley continued, "I chew in the morning, the afternoon, the evening; I love it. If it can be chewed, it's in my mouth."

Oliver stood up. He couldn't believe it, but he wanted to put some distance between himself and Hannah. "Good to know," he said as he backed away. "You might want to think about updating your websites."

"Why?" Miley asked in an overly earnest way. "Does it bother you? It really turns off some people. They can't even be around me. They love me, but I disgust them," she explained.

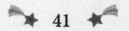

"Well," Oliver announced, "I'm not like that."

Now Miley was getting worried. This *had* to work. "You're not? Because it's okay if you are." She hoped, hoped, hoped that he was like that.

"No," Oliver said decisively. "Relationships are about sacrifice. I accept you . . . just the way you are."

Miley started to freak out. Was it possible that this wasn't working? She had to do something. "Good to know," she said, shovelling another piece of chewing gum into her already stuffed mouth. "Move over, boys. New chew comin' through." She started to chew like a cow, even harder and more disgustingly than even she thought she could.

Oliver was so horrified that he couldn't look away. "Your . . . mouth," he started to say. "It's . . . it's . . ."

"Turning black?" Miley asked brightly. "It's liquorice. My favourite. Just don't make me laugh. It comes out of my nose. Wanna see?"

"No!" Oliver screamed.

"Too late!" Miley yelled. "She's about to blow!" Oliver thought fast and grabbed her nose. He had to keep the black stuff in. It would be too much for him to bear. He loved Hannah, but this was just . . . too much. "Am I grossing you out?" Miley asked. "Because I totally understand if you hate me now and want to transfer your obsession to Mandy Moore. You know, she's blonde again."

Oliver let go of Miley's nose and braced himself for the worst. "No," he said. "My love is bigger than my disgust and your . . . black . . . drippage."

Miley was thoroughly frustrated. This guy wouldn't give up. She had to pull out all the stops. "Speaking of black drippage, check this out!" She started to blow a bubble, a big, black bubble.

Oliver watched in horror. "Sacrifice, sacrifice, sacrifice," he chanted to himself. Miley's bubble started to get out of control. Oliver looked on as it grew and grew, until it could grow no more. Then it burst – right in Oliver's face!

"How do you like me now?" Miley shouted in complete exasperation.

"I ... I ... still love you!" Oliver declared.

Like the big, black bubble, Miley finally exploded. "What does it take with you? What more do I have to do? You and Hannah are never going to be together," she ranted.

"Why not?" Oliver asked.

"Because . . ." Scanning the beach quickly to make sure no one was around, she pulled off her wig and glasses. "I'm Hannah Montana. Me. Miley."

Oliver went stiff, then started to hyperventilate. He promptly passed out.

Miley stared down at him. "Okay, that went well."

Chapter Eight

When Oliver came to, he had a lot of questions for his friend. He paced back and forth in front of her as she sat on the beach, bracing herself for his rampage. "So, you were Hannah Montana in the limo, when I was upside down?" he asked.

"Yes," Miley answered.

"And backstage when I was hanging out of the window?"

"Yep."

"And when I hid in the bass drum and

⭐ Part One

Hannah hits the stage!

"... if he ever finds out your secret, he'll not only be
in love with Hannah Montana,
he'll be in love with *you!*" said Lilly.

"Jackson Stewart, come on down!" Jackson bellowed. "You are the proud new owner of a brand-new used car!"

"Yes," Miley nodded. "I'm definitely seeing a couple here."

"Good luck, Oliver," Lilly bubbled. "But remember, if it doesn't work, you're still 'Smokin' Oken'."

"I love to chew. I chew all the time. Like a train – chew, chew, chew," Miley said.

"I mean, have you ever pictured yourself
buying an island with me, Miley, your friend
the dork?" Miley asked.

"I couldn't get rid of the car, but I did do a
little somethin' to beef it up a bit,"
Mr Stewart said.

Miley interrupted and said, "*Won't* follow Gwen Stefani into the bathroom and ask her to sign a protective seat cover?!"

"I know, I know, but, Lilly – Lola is a really great person once you get to know her," Miley said.

"How do I do it?" Jackson asked
his friend smugly.

Lilly arrived at Miley's dressed in her Lola Luftnagle disguise. She was crushed when Miley told her that the
party had been cancelled.

"She was just trying to even out the sides!" Jackson
yelled defensively.
"It could have happened to anybody."

As Miley left the party, a
photographer approached and yelled,
"Hannah Montana, say 'cheese'!"

"Look who's talking!" Jackson shouted. "I'm not the one taking 'Hannah's Wild Ride'! Weeee!"

"Why is your sofa so lumpy?" Lilly asked.

rode on your tour bus all the way to Phoenix?"

"You did what?" Miley's voice went up an octave in disbelief.

"Nothing." Oliver dismissed her and then stopped pacing. "How could you not tell me?"

"I'm sorry, but you were just so in love with Hannah and I was afraid you might be . . ."

"In love with you? Do you think I am?"

"You tell me. I mean, have you ever pictured yourself buying an island with me, Miley, your friend, the dork?"

"You're not a dork."

"Oh, come on. What about the time I tripped in biology and spilled frog juice all over you?"

"Oh, right, Mum made me take off my trousers in the school car park."

"Or when we were at Andrew's birthday party and you knocked me into the pool in your one-man stampede for the cake?" Miley reminded him.

"That's not fair," Oliver whined. "It was an ice-cream log cake! And you know I have to get an end cut!"

"Okay," Miley said, "what about the time we had to do that scene from *Romeo and Juliet* and you couldn't even kiss me without cringing?"

"Well, those onion rings you ate before class didn't help," Oliver pointed out in his defence.

"Come on, Oliver." Miley was serious now. "Was it the onion rings or was it me?"

Oliver looked at her intently. "I guess it was a little of both," he admitted.

"Oliver, face it," Miley said to her friend. "The girl you thought you loved is standing right here and the truth is, you don't love her."

She had a really good point. Oliver had to take that in for a moment. "Wow," he said. "I think you're right. That's two years of my life I'll never get back."

Miley nodded. "Sorry about that," she said. "So . . . what do you think? Are we gonna be okay?"

"Yeah. We're okay." They looked at each other for a minute, then hugged.

"So, you feel anything?" Miley asked as they hugged.

"Nope," Oliver said, still hugging her. "In fact, it's a little awkward." They broke apart and then regrouped.

"Come on, let's go and grab a hot dog," Miley suggested.

"Sure and you can have all the onions you want," Oliver joked.

As they walked off, Oliver remembered something.

"Hannah," he said. "So, Mandy Moore," he mused. "You don't happen to have her number, do you?"

Miley pretended to be insulted that he had got over her already. "Boy, you bounce back fast," she teased. The two walked happily towards Rico's and all was well again.

Meanwhile, Jackson was still suffering from his bad-car day. He and Cooper were hanging out in the driveway at the Stewarts' house, waiting for Mr Stewart to return with (hopefully) good news. Cooper was busy shooting hoops as Jackson paced and looked at his watch every other second.

"Where is my dad?" he asked, frustrated. "It's been hours. He couldn't sell it. That's what it is. He couldn't sell it and now he can't face me."

Cooper tried to look on the bright side. "You don't know that. Maybe something good happened – maybe he parked it somewhere and a bunch of cheerleaders stole it," he joked.

"Yeah, like I have that kind of luck," Jackson said. Then, just as Jackson had feared, his dad drove up in the same girly car he had left in. "Oh, here he comes. Still driving it. I knew it. Failure! You're a failure as a father!" he shouted.

"Get a grip, son," Mr Stewart said, trying to calm down his hysterical child. "I couldn't get rid of the car, but I did do a little somethin' to beef it up a bit." He honked the horn and out came a blast that an eighteen-wheeler might make. It was the horn of a big rig.

"Dad," Jackson said, "changing the horn's not gonna make it a guy car."

"I know," Mr Stewart admitted, "but this might." Jackson and Cooper watched as Jackson's father pushed a button and the boot popped open. Suddenly, lights started flashing and the stereo started booming. Mr Stewart had customized Jackson's ride and it was cool.

"Dang, this is tight," Cooper admitted.

Mr Stewart was proud of himself. As he got out of the car, he said to Jackson, "Son, I primped your ride."

"Oh, yes, he did!" Cooper yelled.

"Thank you, Dad, thank you!" Jackson jumped up and hugged his father.

"Okay, son, you can let go," Mr Stewart said, extricating himself a little from the hug. Nevertheless, Jackson clung to him tightly, still refusing to let go. "That was cute when you were five," he said. "Now it just throws my back out."

Jackson finally let go, giving his dad a break. But Cooper didn't let Mr Stewart rest for very long.

"My turn!" he shouted as he jumped on Mr Stewart just like Jackson had.

"Yep, there it goes!" Mr Stewart said, reaching for his lower back. Oh, well, at least his children's crises were averted for now. That was all he could ask for!

Part Two

Chapter One

It was a concert night and Miley, dressed as Hannah, was in the middle of a quick, last-minute warm-up with Kay, her vocal coach.

"I'm a lucky girl, whose dreams came true," Hannah sang. "But underneath it all, I'm just like you." She trailed off. "How's that?" she asked Kay.

"Perfect," Kay replied, smiling.

Then they heard the stage manager calling to them. "Hannah Montana, you're on in two minutes," he shouted.

"All right," Kay said seriously. "Shake the nerves out." Hannah shook her shoulders loosely. "Good," Kay said. "Get it out. Loosen up the throat."

Kay told Hannah to do a little vocal exercise and Hannah complied. "Ah, ah, ah, ah . . ." Then Hannah took the shaking to a whole new level – an animal level. She started bouncing and shaking, dancing and screeching . . . like a monkey. Then, just as suddenly as she let the animal take her over, she snapped out of it. "Okay," she said in a completely normal voice, "good to go."

Kay laughed. "Remember when I started coaching you and you were embarrassed to do that?" Kay looked wistful. "I miss those days." She walked off then, leaving Hannah alone. Not long after, two of her 'industry' friends walked in.

"Traci, Evan, I'm so glad you guys are here! You having fun?" she asked her guests, who knew her only as Hannah Montana. Traci and Evan had no idea that Hannah had a whole other *normal* life as Miley Stewart, eighth grader!

"Tons of," Traci replied. Traci was the ultra-hip daughter of Hannah's record producer. She knew everything and everyone. "Except there's this weird girl in your dressing room who keeps sticking her tongue in the chocolate fountain." Traci made a disgusted face.

"She looked like my dog in a rain puddle," Evan chimed in.

"It was a major party foul," Traci said. "Oh, no," she continued, looking in the direction of a disguised Lilly. "There she is."

There she was, all right. Lilly, dressed as her alias, Lola Luftnagle, walked into the

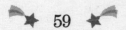

room. As evidence of Traci and Evan's accusations, she had a chocolate ring around her mouth.

"Hannah!" Lilly shouted.

Traci was surprised. "You know her?"

"Look at this," Lilly said, referring to her mobile phone. "I was in the bathroom and got a picture of a very famous finger picking a very famous nose! How great is that?"

Hannah stepped towards her friend and gently closed the offending mobile phone. "Okaaay," she said sarcastically. "Thanks for sharing. Traci and Evan, this is my friend, uh . . ." She had forgotten Lilly's alias! She looked to Lilly, hoping her friend would stop shovelling strawberries into her mouth long enough to help her out. Thankfully, Lilly caught on.

"Lola Luftnagle," she said, with her mouth full. "Daughter of oil baron

Rudolph Luftnagle, sister of socialites Bunny and Kiki Luftnagle, cousin of . . ." Hannah elbowed Lilly in the ribs and she stopped herself. "But you can call me Lola," she said to Traci and Evan, inadvertently spitting some strawberry juice in Traci's face. "Whoops!" she exclaimed. "My fault!"

Traci was less than pleased. "Yes, it is."

Hannah intervened before things got even worse. Stepping between Lilly and Traci, she said, "Soooo, you guys gonna hang backstage?"

"Hey," Lilly shouted. "That'd be cool! We could hang together!" she said to Traci and Evan.

Evan tried to get out of hanging with Lola. "But, then . . . who would sit in our seats?"

"Good point," Traci agreed. "And it is

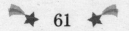 61

getting a little crowded back here."

"I see what you mean," Lilly said, not understanding that Traci was referring to Lilly herself! "Who let some of these people backstage?"

"Really," Traci and Evan said in unison. "Tell me about it." Then, as they walked off, Traci said in a snotty voice, *"Hasta la pasta."* Traci waited until she was out of Hannah and Lilly's range before saying to Evan, "What a loser."

Lilly really had no idea what was going on. "They seem nice. Maybe I should go with them?" Lilly started to walk towards Traci and Evan. Hannah quickly pulled her back.

"Nooo . . . 'cause you're my good-luck charm," she said, wiping Lilly's face with her towel. "My chocolate-covered good-luck charm."

"Whoa," Lilly said, seeing how chocolatey the towel was. "That's embarrassing."

"Oh, you can hardly see it," she tried to reassure her friend. And yet she yelled to the stage manager, "I'm gonna need another towel!"

"Now," she said to Lilly, "I want you to stay right here where I can see you — and no one else will," she said emphatically. "Just pretend those little feet are nailed to the ground."

From the stage, they heard the announcer cry, "Are you ready, San Diego?" The crowd roared. "Then let's hear it! Hannah Montana!" The crowd roared even louder.

Hannah looked seriously at Lilly. "Just nailed right there. Tap, tap, tap."

"Don't worry, 'Hannah'. 'Lola' will be

right here for you," Lilly assured her friend. Hannah headed onto the stage to thunderous applause from her fans and started singing with her signature gusto. Lilly watched her friend, keeping her promise to stay put . . . until . . .

"The bathrooms are over here, Ms Stefani," she heard someone say as a group of people walked by, all surrounding a certain platinum-blonde pop star.

Lilly hesitated at first, but staying put was a lot to ask in this particular situation. "Gwen Stefani!" she yelled, finally running off towards the entourage. "Gwen, babe, wait up. I'll go with you. Why are you running? Gwenny? Gwendela!"

Hannah noticed this from the stage but could do nothing but hope for the best.

Chapter Two

The next day, Miley had a lot on her mind and no one to talk to. There was her dad, asleep on the sofa, his mouth hanging wide open and his guitar leaning on a chair nearby. Miley didn't want to bother him, but she really needed some advice. She decided to be subtle, sitting down next to her father and sighing lightly. Nothing, not a twitch. She sighed again, louder. Still nothing. Time to try something a little more direct.

"Wake up!" she shouted.

Robby Stewart jumped and Miley sighed with relief – her dad was definitely awake now. "Darlin', sometimes I wish you came with a snooze button," he said, shaking off his nap. "Now, what's this all about?"

"Lilly," Miley said dramatically. "I don't know what to say to her. I mean, I don't want to hurt her feelings, but she was so embarrassing backstage." As she spoke, Jackson, Miley's older brother, came down the stairs and grabbed some popcorn.

"How bad was it?" Mr Stewart asked, referring to Lilly's backstage behaviour.

Jackson happily piped up. "Let's just say Lilly made a little unscheduled trip last night to Dork Flats, Iowa. Population: her," he said as he headed for the kitchen.

Mr Stewart followed his son while he calmed Miley. "Come on, Mile, she's just not used to being backstage. I'm sure next time she—"

Miley interrupted her father and said, "*Won't* follow Gwen Stefani into the bathroom and ask her to sign her protective seat cover?!" Miley's dad and brother started laughing. "It ain't funny," she said to them.

Mr Stewart put on a serious face. "No, it's not," he said, looking at Jackson, "What's wrong with you, boy?"

Miley was exasperated. "You just don't know what it's like to have someone you love embarrass you all the time." The conversation came to a halt as Miley and her dad watched Jackson pour a heaping spoonful of powdered chocolate into his mouth, then swig a big gulp of milk and shake his head to mix them together, while jumping up and down for good measure.

Then, at last, he swallowed his 'chocolate milk'.

"Oh, I think I do," Mr Stewart said to Miley.

The phone rang and Jackson answered it, his mouth still thick with his concoction. "Hello?" He hung up the phone, then said to Miley and Mr Stewart, "Lilly landing in three . . . two . . . one."

As usual, Miley opened the front door just as Lilly sailed in on her skateboard. "That concert last night was so much fun. I had so much fun. Did you have so much fun?" Lilly asked as she skidded to a halt in the kitchen.

Jackson put on his best girl voice and started to mock his sister. "I had fun! Did you see the dreamy boy in the third row? Woo!"

"We do not sound like that!" Miley

insisted to her brother. "And he was in the second row."

As Jackson and Miley argued, Lilly re-enacted the very same chocolate-milk-making method Jackson had displayed just moments before. Mr Stewart walked over and took the milk away from Lilly after she had swigged it. "Come on, people, I make pancakes with that milk!" he complained.

At that moment, the distinctive ringtone of Hannah Montana's mobile phone filled the room.

"Yes!" Lilly exclaimed. "The Hannah line – it's always somebody so cool! Let me answer it this time!" she begged.

"No, no, I'll get it," Miley said as she flipped her phone open. "Yo-la!" Miley said as she put the phone to her ear. Lilly wouldn't give up. She moved close to the phone and put her ear to the other side of it. Even as Miley moved away from her friend, Lilly followed.

It was Traci on the line. "Hey, superstar, it's Trace."

"What's going on?" Miley asked.

"We're throwing a little birthday party for Kelly tonight—"

"Kelly?" Lilly asked. "Kelly Clarkson?" Again, Miley tried to move away from Lilly, to no avail.

Traci continued, "And if you don't come, I'll get all pouty."

"Ahhh!" Lilly shouted gleefully. "This is so cool. We're going to Kel-*lay*'s par-*tay*!" She started to dance in celebration.

Miley covered the mouthpiece and looked at her jig-dancing friend. "What are you doing?" she asked Lilly.

"I'm doing my 'I'm going to Kel-*lay*'s par-*tay*' dance," Lilly replied.

Still covering the phone, Miley said, "And I love it. It's just that . . . I'm not sure I can take anybody with me."

"Well, ask her," Lilly insisted.

"Ask her. Yes. I should do that."

"Now!" Lilly demanded.

"Now. Yes. I should do that . . . now."

Lilly jammed her head next to Miley's as Miley asked Traci questions. "So, Trace . . . I can't bring anybody, right?" She prayed for a no, even as Lilly was praying just as hard for a yes.

"Sure, Kelly said you can bring anybody you want," Traci said, confirming Miley's fear.

Lilly, on the other hand, was ecstatic. "Yes!" she yelled right into the phone. "Trace, it's Lola! I'll see you there!"

Sitting in the recording studio on her mobile phone, Traci said back to Lola,

"Loving it." Then she too covered the phone and said to herself, "Hating her."

"This is so cool. I can't believe I'm actually going to a big Hollywood party!" Lilly said. "Excuse me." Lilly walked out to the porch and closed the door behind her. They all watched as she did her happy dance outside.

Traci, however, was not doing a happy dance. "Hannah, I have a micro problem," she said.

"I know, I know, but Lilly – Lola is a really great person once you get to know her." Miley was trying to plead her friend's case.

"Yeah, see, the getting-to-know-her part? That's the problem," Traci replied. Miley braced herself for what she knew was coming. "I mean, she's just so uncool, it's totally embarrassing."

"Yeah, but–" Miley wanted to stand up for Lilly, but Traci cut her off.

"I knew you'd understand. *Ciao*." Then the line went dead.

Miley didn't know what to do. She headed for the kitchen where Mr Stewart and Jackson were eating cake – her dad with a fork, her brother with his hands.

"Lilly's not invited, is she?" Mr Stewart asked.

Miley put her head on her dad's shoulder. "What am I gonna do? Look–" she directed them to Lilly, who was still dancing on the porch. "And that's her before the party. I just wish there was a magic spell that could stop people from acting like . . . geeksicles!"

As Mr Stewart watched his son try to catapult a marshmallow into his mouth with a spoon, he agreed. "Me too."

Chapter Three

Later that day, Jackson was working at Rico's, serving Miley's friend Oliver and his co-worker and friend Rico some lunch, when a beautiful girl walked into the restaurant. Though the girl smiled at the group, Oliver 'Mr Confidence' Oken stepped right up. "Whoa, older woman, checking me out," he said.

"In your dreams, Oken," Jackson sneered.

Oliver had to concede that point. "Normally, yes, but–"

"She's only lookin' at you," Jackson interrupted, "'cause you're sitting next to me."

"*Playas*, please," Rico said, stepping in. "I'm the man she wants. I'm cute, I'm rich—"

"And you would fit in her handbag." Jackson couldn't resist. His friend Rico was tiny! "*Muy macho*!"

"Watch and learn, boys," Oliver said, confident that he was in the running for the girl's attention. "But don't applaud; it might embarrass her."

Jackson rolled his eyes. He and Rico watched Oliver swagger over to the girl.

"Hi," he said quietly. "Could you just pretend to want to talk to me? My friends are watching."

"Oh, I don't have to pretend," she answered, much to Oliver's surprise.

"You're cute."

"Really?"

The girl took Oliver's face in her hands and said in a high-pitched baby voice, "Yes you are. You're the cutest little boy. Look at that face," she squealed as she pinched his cheeks. "And those chubby, chubby cheeks!"

Oliver pulled away, mortified. "Okay, not helping!"

"I'm sorry," she said, still using that sugary voice. "Let me make it all better. Do you want some sweets?"

Would the embarrassment never end? "No, I don't want any swee–" He paused, intrigued. "What kind is it?" He peeked in her bag and took out a chocolate bar. Satisfied with himself, Oliver marched back to his friends. Jackson and Rico were cracking up.

"Laugh it up, boys," Oliver said. "I got sweets on the first date." Then he walked away, content to eat his free chocolate bar.

It was Rico's turn now. He turned to Jackson after Oliver left. "Well, now it's time for a real man. It's 'Rico time'." True to form, he then licked his fingers and used them to smooth his eyebrows.

"Yeah," Jackson replied. "It's Rico's bedtime," he said as he hopped over the serving counter to step ahead of his rival. He looked back at Rico on his way to the older woman. "Get ready to cry yourself to sleep."

Jackson, like Oliver, walked confidently up to the girl and said, "Hi, please pretend to like me, my boss's kid is watching."

"But I do like you," she said.

Thinking she was simply helping a guy out, Jackson said, "That's perfect, just a little more–" He paused, noticing that she seemed to be serious. "Oh."

"I'm Nina," she said.

Jackson happily shook her hand. "Jackson," he said. He couldn't believe this was happening. This girl was gorgeous. Way out of his league. Even he had to admit that.

"Look, I don't mean to be pushy–" Nina continued.

"No, please, push," Jackson insisted. "I like pushy. Pushy is good."

"I'm a student at the Malibu School of Beauty, and I was wondering if I could borrow your head?" Nina asked.

"What?"

"It's just that your hair is so fantastic and I really need someone to practise on and I'd give just anything to get my hands on it," she gushed.

"Well, it's your lucky day, anything is

exactly my price." Jackson didn't care what she wanted to do with his hair. Any time spent with Nina would be just fine with him. He led her to the serving counter. "Have a seat," he said.

As he crossed over to his side of the counter, he grinned at Rico. "How do I do it?" he asked his friend smugly.

Nina and Rico looked at each other knowingly, as if they knew something Jackson didn't. "You got me," Rico said quietly, laughing a silly, evil laugh. "Or, I got you."

Back at the Stewart household later that day, Jackson started to understand what Rico's evil laugh had been about. Sitting in the middle of his kitchen in a barber's chair, draped with a smock, Jackson stared at himself in a hand mirror.

"Wow. That's . . . interesting," he stammered. He had orange hair – bright orange hair. What else was there to say?

"I'm so sorry. My parents were right. I don't have what it takes to be a beautician." Nina was practically in tears.

"Of course you do," Jackson reassured her. He couldn't get too angry. She was too pretty. "Don't worry, we can fix this. We can fix this, right?"

"Yeah, let me just go home and practise on my dog one more time. I'll see you tomorrow," she said hurriedly as she got ready to leave.

"Tomorrow?! But what about–"

"You're so sweet and understanding," Nina swooned. She leaned down and kissed him on the forehead, which truly made everything much better for Jackson.

"No worries, I have hats," he said.

Just as Nina ran out, Mr Stewart walked in. He spotted Jackson's new look right away. "Don't start," Jackson said to his father.

"It's okay, son. Heck, I've done my share of crazy things to get in with a girl." He looked harder at his son's head. "Nothing as . . . orange as that. See, in my day we had a little thing called pride."

"In your day, you had a little thing called a mullet," Jackson retorted.

"And it was a thing of beauty. Business at the front, party at the back." Mr Stewart got lost in the memory for a moment, until he realized that his son wasn't laughing. He walked over to Jackson and put his arms around him. "Listen, from what I can tell, she's a really nice girl. Just keep your eye on the prize."

Mr Stewart went out, leaving Jackson

there alone. Only he wasn't really alone. Peeking in at the window was Rico, who was very proud of himself. If Jackson had turned around just then, he would have seen Rico laughing that evil laugh and rubbing his hands in celebration. Instead, Jackson just felt an eerie chill as a flash of lightning lit up Rico's creepy face lurking at the window.

Chapter Four

Later that day, Jackson was hanging out in the kitchen, pondering his new carrot top, when Miley came in. She was dressed as Hannah, in preparation for the big party.

"Hey, shouldn't you be at that party?" Jackson asked his sister.

"I'm going. I just have to tell Lilly the truth first. I know it's gonna be hard, but it's the right thing to do." Miley was dreading telling her friend the news.

Suddenly, Jackson let out a big, dramatic, "No! No! It hurts so baaaaad!"

"What are you doing?" Miley asked.

"An imitation of Lilly in about two minutes," Jackson replied, as if he knew everything. "Now if you want to avoid that, here's a little tip from your big brother: lie like a rug."

"Yeah, I'm really gonna take advice from a guy who looks like a traffic cone." Miley couldn't resist mocking her know-it-all brother. Besides, he had orange hair. He *did* look like a traffic cone.

But Jackson was quick with a comeback, as always. "Traffic cones save lives," he said on his way out. Miley shook her head at her brother and went to the front door to greet Lilly. Ah, Lilly. There she was when Miley opened the door. Dressed as Lola, she danced in a one-girl conga line into the living room.

"Par-*tay*, par-*tay*, par-*tay*!" she sang. "Par-*tay*, par-*tay*, par-*tay*! Everybody now! Par-*tay*, par-*tay*, par–" Lilly paused, finally noticing that Miley was not joining in with the enthusiasm she expected. In fact, Miley was not joining in at all. "Hey, what's wrong?"

Miley took a deep breath and said, "Lilly, we have to talk."

Lilly shrugged this off. "Well, let's talk on the way to the par-*tay*," she suggested.

"No, Lilly, we have to talk now," Miley said firmly. She took her friend's arm and urged her over towards the sofa.

Now Lilly was visibly concerned. "Why? What's the matter?" she asked as they sat down.

"Okay, we've always promised to be honest with each other, right?" Miley asked, hoping that this conversation was going to go well.

"Yeah," Lilly said.

"No matter how hard that might be," Miley continued.

Lilly was very worried now. "Are you trying to tell me that this shirt doesn't go with these trousers?" she asked with alarm in her voice.

Miley paused to think about this. "Yes," she said. The trousers didn't go at all. "But also . . . okay, I'm just going to say it. The truth is . . ." She saw the concern in Lilly's face and couldn't go through with it. "The party's cancelled," she said instead.

Lilly was crushed, of course, but not nearly as crushed as she would have been had Miley actually told her the truth. Miley just couldn't do that to her friend. However, she couldn't miss the party, either, so after Lilly went home to study, Miley headed to the party . . . alone.

Miley waited outside for her dad to pick her up from the club where the party was being held. She had gone in, but she just didn't feel right. Her guilt was eating her up with every celebrity she spotted. Poor Lilly. Miley was almost free and clear, when Traci spotted her.

"Hannah, I've been looking all over for you. What are you doing out here?" she asked.

"I'm waiting for my dad to pick me up," she answered, trying to sound casual.

"But Kelly's not even here yet," Traci pleaded.

"I know, but I guess I'm just not feeling in a party mood tonight," she said.

"Okay, love you, but you're downin' my

vibe. T-T-Y-L." And she was off, heading back into the club. It was just like Traci not to care why 'Hannah' wasn't in a party mood. Just then, Miley's mobile phone rang, and before she thought to check the caller ID, she answered it.

"Hello?"

"So, whatcha doing?" It was Lilly. Of course it was Lilly.

"Lilly?! Um . . ." Miley had to think fast. Why had she answered? "I'm not doing anything. Nothing. Just . . . studying. No party. Just me. Party of one." Could it be any worse than this? And of course, the door to the club opened at that very moment and there was a loud hiss of music and crowd noise.

"What's that?" Lilly asked.

"Oh. That's . . ." She closed the door herself. "That's just Jackson playing his stereo too loud." She pretended to shout to Jackson. "Jackson, turn it down! I'm studying, fool!" Then, when she saw how the bouncer outside the door was looking at her, she whispered to him, "Sorry, not you. Nice nose ring."

Lilly didn't seem fazed. "So, you want to go to the mall tomorrow?" she asked cheerfully.

"Sure, sounds like fun," Miley answered, relieved that Lilly wasn't more suspicious. But, just as relief set in, some paparazzi approached and yelled, "Hannah Montana, say 'cheese'!" Oh, that's just *perfect*, Miley thought.

"Who's that?" Lilly asked.

"My dad . . ." Miley said, hoping Lilly would buy this one, too. Then she pretended to yell back to her dad, "No, Dad, I don't want extra cheese!" But the paparazzi wouldn't give up. She noticed that they were taking her picture. "I gotta hang up," she said to Lilly, "before he goes all deep-pan on me."

Miley had to nip this one in the bud. Her lie would be exposed if someone printed those pictures and Lilly saw them, which she definitely would, since Lilly read every celebrity magazine and newspaper there was. She approached the photographers. "Hi," she said sweetly. "I have a friend who can't know that I'm here, so I was wondering if y'all could be good guys and not print that picture."

"Sure, sweetheart, no problem," one photographer said, as if he was going to comply. "Oh, wait, I'm not a good guy." The photographer thought his little joke was pretty funny. He laughed and snapped yet another picture of her.

He turned to walk away, but Miley was fed up. "Well, in that case, I'm not a good girl." With that, she jumped on his back and tried to grab the camera out of his hands. Well, this struggle attracted quite a bit of attention — just the kind of attention Miley was trying to avoid! Miley looked up to see a hail of flashbulbs explode in her face. And to make matters worse, there was a video crew capturing the whole thing. This was not going to be good.

Chapter Five

It was even worse than Miley had thought. Her picture was plastered across the front page of the L.A. *Herald*'s entertainment section. HANNAH'S WILD RIDE was the headline and the picture wasn't pretty. Miley had a lot of work to do. There was no way she could let Lilly see the paper. It was irrational, but she set out to gather every copy of the *Herald* she could find, so that Lilly wouldn't spot the story.

Meanwhile, at the Stewart home, Jackson was defending yet another disaster, courtesy of the world's worst beauty-school student. Now Jackson was sporting a blue mohican! When Mr Stewart walked in from his run, Jackson was quick to preempt his father's jokes. "She was just trying to even out the sides!" he yelled defensively. "It could have happened to anybody."

"I'm not going to say a thing," Mr Stewart replied.

"Thank you." Jackson was grateful that his dad was willing to let this one go.

"I'm going to sing a thing," Mr Stewart said and then he started singing. "I once knew a girl named Nina and was she a find. So I gave my sweetie my golden locks. Now I look like a bluebird's behind." Then he started to really belt it out. "Bluebird's behind, bluebird's behind . . ."

Jackson didn't appreciate this one bit. "Whatever happened to using your own misery to write a song?" he asked.

"I'm sorry, son, I only make fun 'cause I went through it myself. Every man has. At least you can take some comfort in the fact that you got yourself a date with a pretty girl," Mr Stewart offered.

"Well, not yet," Jackson admitted.

"Ouch," Mr Stewart said.

Miley entered just in time to save Jackson from more mocking. She had an armful of newspapers. "Okay," she said. "That's all the papers between Lilly's house and here." Then she spotted her brother's new do. "Good Lord! How desperate are you?" The phone rang and Mr Stewart left his bickering kids to answer it.

"Look who's talking!" Jackson shouted, holding up one of the papers Miley had collected. "I'm not the one taking 'Hannah's Wild Ride'! Weeee!"

"Listen, schmuck, if Lilly finds out why I didn't take her to that party, it'll crush her. I'm not gonna let that happen." Miley was serious. She couldn't stand the thought of hurting Lilly.

Mr Stewart interrupted. "Then you might want to make those newspapers disappear, because – Lilly in ten."

Miley started running around like a wild woman, scrambling to hide the papers under the sofa cushions. "Don't just stand there!" she yelled. "I need tushes! Quick!" She grabbed Jackson and her dad and dragged them over to the sofa, where they planted themselves on the goods. Miley ran to the door to intercept Lilly.

"You ready?" Lilly asked Miley when she met her at the door.

Miley was confused. "For what?"

"The mall. I've got to pick out a slammin' outfit for the next party. I mean, I wouldn't want to embarrass you," Lilly answered.

"Right. Wouldn't want that," Miley said nervously. "Let's go to the mall."

But as they headed for the front door, Jackson spoke up. "The good old mall," he said, "with that big news-stand and all those people talking about what's in the news and who's in the news and—"

Miley took the hint and redirected Lilly, who was still on her skateboard, to the back door. "On the other hand, the beach sounds fun, too," she said.

"But the mall has cute clothes," Lilly protested.

"But the beach has cute boys."

That did it. "To the beach!" Lilly sang.

Miley and Lilly's day at the beach included a stop at the shower platform, where they could watch the cute guys walk by. They were doing just that when Oliver yelled to them.

"Guys!" Oliver yelled. "You'll never guess who made the cover of the entertainment section!" He was waving a newspaper wildly.

Miley had to think fast. She grabbed a football from one of the guys passing by.

"Wait! Oliver, catch!" she shouted, throwing the football as far out of Oliver's reach as she could.

Oliver dived for the ball, shouting, "Too far!" as he fell out of sight.

"Come on, I'm hungry," Miley said to Lilly, dragging her over to the snack bar. But there was no relief anywhere. An old lady sitting next to them was reading a newspaper with the entertainment-section cover facing out. Miley grabbed a mustard bottle and squirted it all over the front page of the woman's paper. Lilly noticed what Miley had done and Miley panicked. She snatched the paper out of the woman's hands and furiously began folding and smashing it. It was a sight to behold.

She looked at the puzzled woman apologetically and said, "There was a bee." She looked at Lilly. "Big bee," she said to her confused friend. "I think I got it," she said to the woman. A bedraggled Oliver walked over, trading one awkward moment for another. This was getting exhausting for Miley.

"Okay," Oliver panted. "Seriously, I want you guys to see this!" he shouted, still clutching the newspaper.

"Uh . . ." Miley stalled. She noticed a guy carrying a surfboard and got an idea. "Hey, dude with the board!" she called. The guy turned, just as Miley knew he would and hit Oliver with the board, sending him flying again. "Never mind!" she yelled to the surfer. "You know what?" she said to Lilly. "It's too crowded here. Hey! Let's go and look for sea glass!" The two headed back out to the beach . . . away from all the newspapers!

"Okay," Nina said to Jackson, who was once again sitting in a makeshift barber's chair in the middle of the kitchen. He had a towel wrapped around his head and Nina was about to unveil her latest attempt. "I think I fixed it. Cross your fingers."

Jackson crossed his fingers, toes and anything else he could cross as Nina whipped off the towel. "Why do I feel a breeze on my head? Why do I feel my head?" he asked, feeling his newly bald head with his hand. Nina held up a mirror so Jackson could see the result of her work. Meanwhile, Rico watched slyly from the window. "Well, at least I know you've finished." Rico heard this, laughed, and walked off feeling very satisfied with himself. "But . . . it's okay," Jackson continued. "When it grows back you can try again."

Nina was shocked. "You'd really let me try again?" she asked.

"Sure," Jackson shrugged. "Meanwhile, we could go to a movie . . . where no one can see me."

Nina was exasperated. "I can't take this any more. You're bald! Why aren't you cross with me?"

"Well, it's not like you did it on purpose," Jackson said.

"But I did!" Nina yelled.

Jackson was floored. "Why? Why would anyone—" Jackson paused, thinking for a minute. Then a lightbulb went off in his head. "Oh, no, something smells like Rico," he groaned.

"The kid paid me," Nina finally admitted. "I never would've done it if I'd known you were so nice. I just wish I could help you get him back."

"I'm sorry, I'm just too upset to think about revenge right now," Jackson said drearily. He perked up pretty fast, though. "Okay, I'm over it."

The two of them plotted their revenge and headed over to Rico's. Jackson hid nearby while Nina convinced Rico he needed a little haircut of his own. As

Jackson had learned, she was pretty convincing! Rico happily obliged. He sat down in a chair and let Nina put a smock on him. Rico was so excited about the successful trick he had played on Jackson that he had to hear all the details.

"Tell me again what Jackson looked like when he realized it was me," he begged.

Nina made her best frightened face, pretending to mock Jackson's reaction.

"And don't forget the scream," Rico reminded her. "That's my favourite part."

Nina let out a piercing scream.

"Life just doesn't get any better than this," Rico gloated.

"You got it. Just close your eyes, sit back and relax," Nina told him.

Rico complied, closing his eyes and relaxing to the buzzing sound of Nina's electric hair clippers. What he didn't see was Nina handing her clippers to Jackson, who had sneaked in and taken over. "Not too much off the sides now," Rico said, eyes still closed.

"Mmm-hmmm," Jackson hummed in as high-pitched a voice as he could.

Chapter Six

It was later that day, much later, when Miley and Lilly got back to the Stewart house. Miley had kept Lilly out collecting sea glass all afternoon and into the evening. It was the only way she could keep her away from the news.

"Wow, I've got enough sea glass to make a coffee table," Miley announced to Lilly. "How about you?"

"I've got enough sea glass to never, ever look for it again," she answered. Then she noticed a newspaper lying out. "Oh, are the comics here? We didn't get our paper today. Nobody on our street did."

Miley dived over the sofa and grabbed the paper out of Lilly's hands. She had gone through too much today to have Lilly find out now. "Oh, who cares about the comics?" she questioned dramatically. "Fat, lazy cats, that pumpkin-headed kid who's always trying to kick the football – boring! Let's just talk – we never talk." She was rambling.

"We talked all day," Lilly said.

"Good point. I'm sick of my own voice." Miley turned on the television. "Let's hear someone else's." But the TV betrayed her.

"Coming up on *This Week in Hollywood*," the voice on the television blared, "*what pouty pop princess pummelled a paparazzi–*" Miley turned the TV off and threw

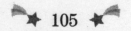

the remote over her shoulder out of Lilly's reach.

"Bad idea!" Miley shouted.

"But I wanted to see that!" Lilly complained. She was distracted, though. She bounced on the sofa, noting that something was strange about it. "Why is your sofa so lumpy?"

"Ooh! Speaking of lumpy – let's make some porridge," Miley suggested, in a misguided attempt to deceive her friend yet again. She dragged Lilly into the kitchen. "Nothing like a big, hot bowl of porridge after a long day at the beach." Just then, the Hannah line rang, but the phone was nowhere near Miley.

"Ooh, the Hannah phone!" Lilly announced. "Can I get it?"

"No!" Miley yelled.

"Wrong answer!" Lilly said as she

grabbed the phone before Miley could get there. "Hello, Hannah Montana's close personal friend Lola here . . ." Lilly paused to listen. "Oh, my gosh, Kelly!" She covered the phone and looked at Miley. "It's actually Kelly! On your actual phone!" She put on a posh accent and returned to the phone. "*Hellooooo . . .*"

"Give me the phone," Miley demanded, chasing Lilly.

But Lilly would not give it up. "So, Kelly-belly, I'm sorry your party was cancelled."

"Come on, Lilly," Miley whined nervously, "give it!"

"What do you mean?" Lilly asked Kelly, puzzled. "Hannah said . . ."

Miley was desperate. "Don't listen to her!" she said to Lilly. "She doesn't like me! Professional jealousy! Petty, petty girl!"

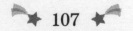

Lilly turned to face Miley. "Okay," she said to Kelly sombrely, "I'll tell her you called." Then she hung up the phone.

"Lilly," Miley said. "I can explain . . . I didn't tell you about the party because—"

"You didn't want me there," Lilly said.

"No, it wasn't me that didn't want you there, it was . . . everybody else," Miley admitted.

"But I thought they liked me," Lilly said.

Miley had to tell her the truth now. It was all she had left. "Actually, they thought you were kind of . . . uncool."

"Even after you told them how cool I was?" Lilly saw how guilty Miley looked and realized what was going on. "You didn't tell them, did you?"

"Not exactly," Miley answered.

"Why?" Lilly was hurt.

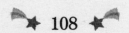

"It doesn't matter why. You don't need them for friends. Isn't it enough that I'm your friend?" Miley pleaded.

"If you're really my friend, you'll tell me the truth," Lilly reminded her.

"Okay . . ." Miley steeled herself. She knew she had to tell Lilly how she was feeling, but she also knew how hard it would be for her to hear. "You spat food on people, you followed them into bathrooms and you walked around with a chocolate beard. Lilly . . ." She didn't know what she was going to say next, but Lilly interrupted her anyway.

"I get it," she said, accepting the blame. "You were embarrassed by me."

"I'm sorry," Miley said. It was all she could say.

"Oh, man, I can't believe I acted like such a dork," Lilly lamented. "Why do I always do that? Lilly, when are you ever gonna learn?" she asked herself out loud as she collapsed onto the sofa.

"Don't be so hard on yourself. The first time I saw a chocolate fountain, I got so excited I poured half of it into my handbag," Miley reassured her friend.

"You're just saying that to make me feel better." Lilly was on to Miley.

"I know. But—" As she was talking, Lilly pulled a newspaper out from under the sofa cushions.

"What's this?" Lilly asked with a puzzled look on her face. She opened the paper to the entertainment section and finally caught a glimpse of the picture Miley had been jumping through hoops to hide all day.

"I kinda got caught leaving the party early," Miley admitted.

"Why were you leaving early?" Lilly asked.

Miley paused and looked at Lilly sweetly. "'Cause it was no fun without you . . . and you know what? That's never gonna happen again."

The next night Miley and Lilly got all dressed up in their Hannah and Lola gear and showed up at the Cobra Room, the club where Traci would be hanging out. As they approached the door, Lilly said, "Miley, I told you, you don't have to do this, we're still best friends."

"Not if I don't do this." Miley was determined to right the wrong she'd done to Lilly. Just then, Traci appeared and approached them.

"Hannah, it's so awesome to see you with . . . her," she said in her snobbiest

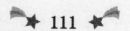

tone. "What was it again? Lola Loser-Nagle?"

Miley was angry. "It's Luftnagle!" At least she hoped it was. She looked at Lilly. "It *is* Luftnagle, right?"

"I think," Lilly responded with a shrug.

"Well, whatever it is," Traci grumbled, "she's not on the list. Right, Derek?" She looked at the bouncer for backup.

"I don't really care," he said. "Why do people think I care?"

"Because my daddy is the hottest record producer in town," Traci whined.

"Now I care. Can I give you my demo?" Derek asked eagerly as he pulled a CD from his jacket. "It's country."

Traci took the CD from him. "Of course!" she said, faking a smile. "Okay," she said, looking at Miley, "yes." Then, she turned to Lilly. "No. 'Nuff said."

Lilly pulled away and looked at Miley. "You go, I'll just call my mum."

"No way," Miley commanded. She looked seriously at Traci. "I like you, Trace, but if you wanna be my friend, she's part of the deal."

Traci pulled Miley aside and whispered, "But she's just so uncool."

"Not as uncool as you were when you shot a snot rocket so big it hit the Olsen Twins," she reminded Traci.

Traci was mortified by the memory. "That's not fair. You know I have sinus problems."

"Everybody has problems. But a good friend doesn't bail on you when you have them," Miley lectured. "I didn't bail on you with the twins and I'm not bailing on Lilly."

"Lola," Lilly volunteered.

"Right," Miley said.

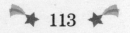

"Okay, fine," Traci conceded, turning towards Lilly. "But tell anybody about the snot rocket and you're out."

"Deal," Lilly agreed.

"Meet you in there," Traci said to both of them as she headed back inside. Then Miley and Lilly heard a stifled sniffle and turned to see Derek the bouncer wiping away a tear.

"What you did for your friend was real nice," he said to Miley.

"I think so, too," Lilly said to Miley.

Miley couldn't help but blush. "There you go, embarrassing me again." The girls smiled at each other sweetly. Then the door of the club opened again as a woman left. Lilly peeked in and caught a glimpse of something – or someone – that got her going.

"Is that Orlando Bloom?" she yelled.

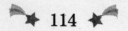

Then she remembered her vow. "I'm cool. I'm cool," she said . . . coolly.

"Oh, just go for it," Miley said.

"Thanks!" Lilly said, dashing inside.

Derek looked at Miley. "She is kind of a dork."

Miley smiled. "I know. But she's my dork." She headed inside to join Lilly, yelling, "Orlando!" If you can't beat 'em, join 'em. All was well with Miley and Lilly, and it was time to par-*tay*!

Joining 'em was the theme of the evening for Jackson and Rico, too. Back at Rico's, Jackson was fighting off all the sniggers about his bald head. His current customer was no exception. He sniggered as Jackson handed him a hot dog.

"That's real smart. Laugh at the person who handles your food!" Jackson shouted, a little worked up.

"You tell 'em, cue ball," Rico said. Rico was sitting there, bald as an eagle as well.

"Thanks, Mini-Me," Jackson said. "You know, I think what we've learned is that there are no winners in a war like this. Only hairless casualties."

"You're right," Rico agreed. "Maybe we should call a truce. Deal?"

"Deal," Jackson said.

They each picked up a can of pop, then toasted their new friendship.

"To peace," Rico offered.

"To harmony," Jackson returned. But they both had other plans for each other, as usual. One grabbed a bottle of mustard and the other a bottle of ketchup. It was on! As Jackson and Rico squirted each other, they couldn't help but acknowledge the other's skills in the practical jokes department.

"Touché!" they said in unison. If not the best of friends, they certainly were worthy adversaries.